Happy
HARRY'S
Café

For Emma, Elsie, and Emile, and remembering my father, Harold, who told me a version of this story
M. R.

For Camilla and Evie   R. H.

Text copyright © 2012 by Michael Rosen
Illustrations copyright © 2012 by Richard Holland

First U.S. edition 2012

Library of Congress Cataloging-in-Publication Data is available.

Library of Congress Catalog Card Number pending

ISBN 978-0-7636-6239-4

12 13 14 15 16 17 SCP 10 9 8 7 6 5 4 3 2 1

Printed in Humen, Donngguan, China

This book was typeset in Bodoni Poster Compressed.
The illustrations were done in mixed media.

Candlewick Press
99 Dover Street
Somerville, Massachusetts 02144

visit us at www.candlewick.com

Michael Rosen

Happy
HARRY'S
Café

illustrated by

Richard Holland

CANDLEWICK PRESS

Here's
Harry.
He works at
Happy
HARRY'S
Café.

Harry makes great

soup.

His friends come running for Harry's

soup

before Harry's

soup

runs out.

Here's **Ryan** the lion.

He's in a rush. He's Rushing Ryan.

"Take it easy, Ryan," says Harry.

Here's
Jo the crow.

She's riding fast.

Jo's no Slow-Jo—oh, no.

"Take it easy, Jo," says Harry.

Here's
Robin the robin.

Robin is really bobbing along.

"Take it easy, Robin," says Harry.

Here's
Matt the cat.

As fast as the wind, and faster than that.

"Take it easy, Matt," says Harry.

They're all in a hurry to have Harry's

soup.

Everyone loves Harry's

soup.

Daily Meow

WANTED
$1000
REWARD

"Love the soup, Harry. **Yum!**"

"Mmmmm!"

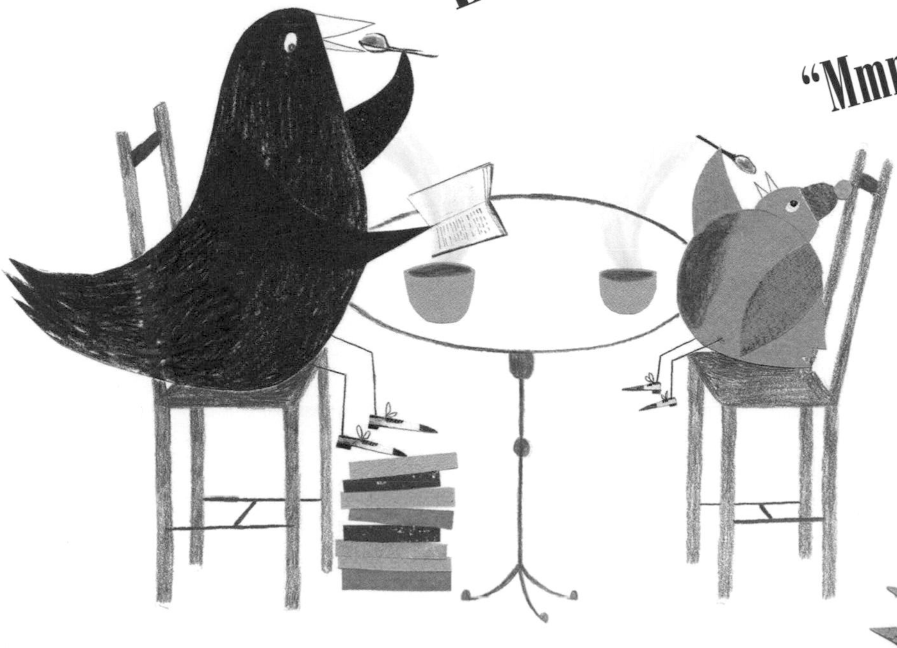

"Great soup, Harry.

Terrific!"

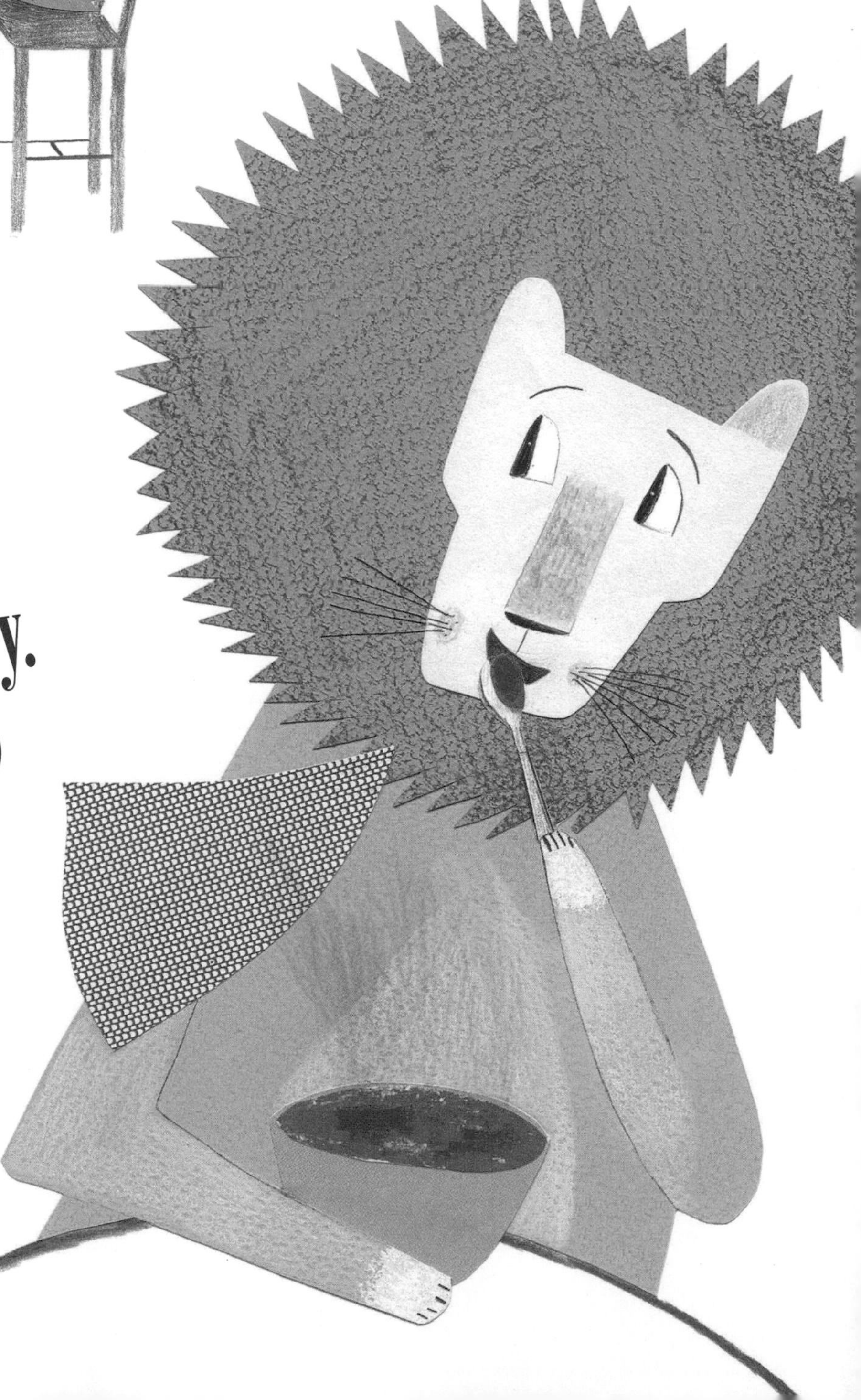

Harry is happy.
He's Happy Harry.

But what about Matt?
Something's wrong with Matt.

"Hey,
Harry,"
says Matt.
"The
soup's
no good."

WANTED
$1000
REWARD

Daily Meow

"WHAT?"

says
Harry.
"Everyone
loves my
soup."

"You come and try it,

Harry,"

says Matt.

"OK, Matt,"

says

Harry.

"I'll try it."

"Hey, Matt," says Harry. "There's no spoon. You haven't got a spoon."

"That's it, Harry!"

says Matt.

"There's no spoon.

I haven't got a spoon.

That's what's wrong with the

soup,

Harry."

Everyone laughs about the **soup** with no spoon.

Ha Ha Ha!

Ha Ha!

Ha Ha!

Ha Ha Ha!

Ha Ha Ha!

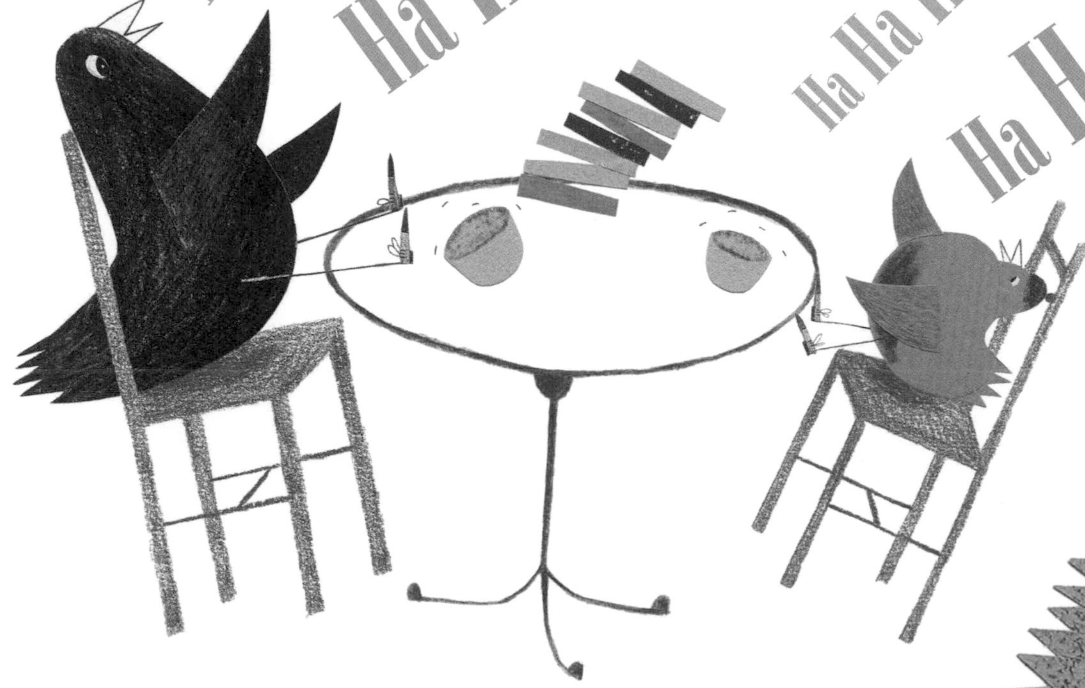

Ha Ha Ha!

Ha Ha Ha!

Ha Ha Ha!

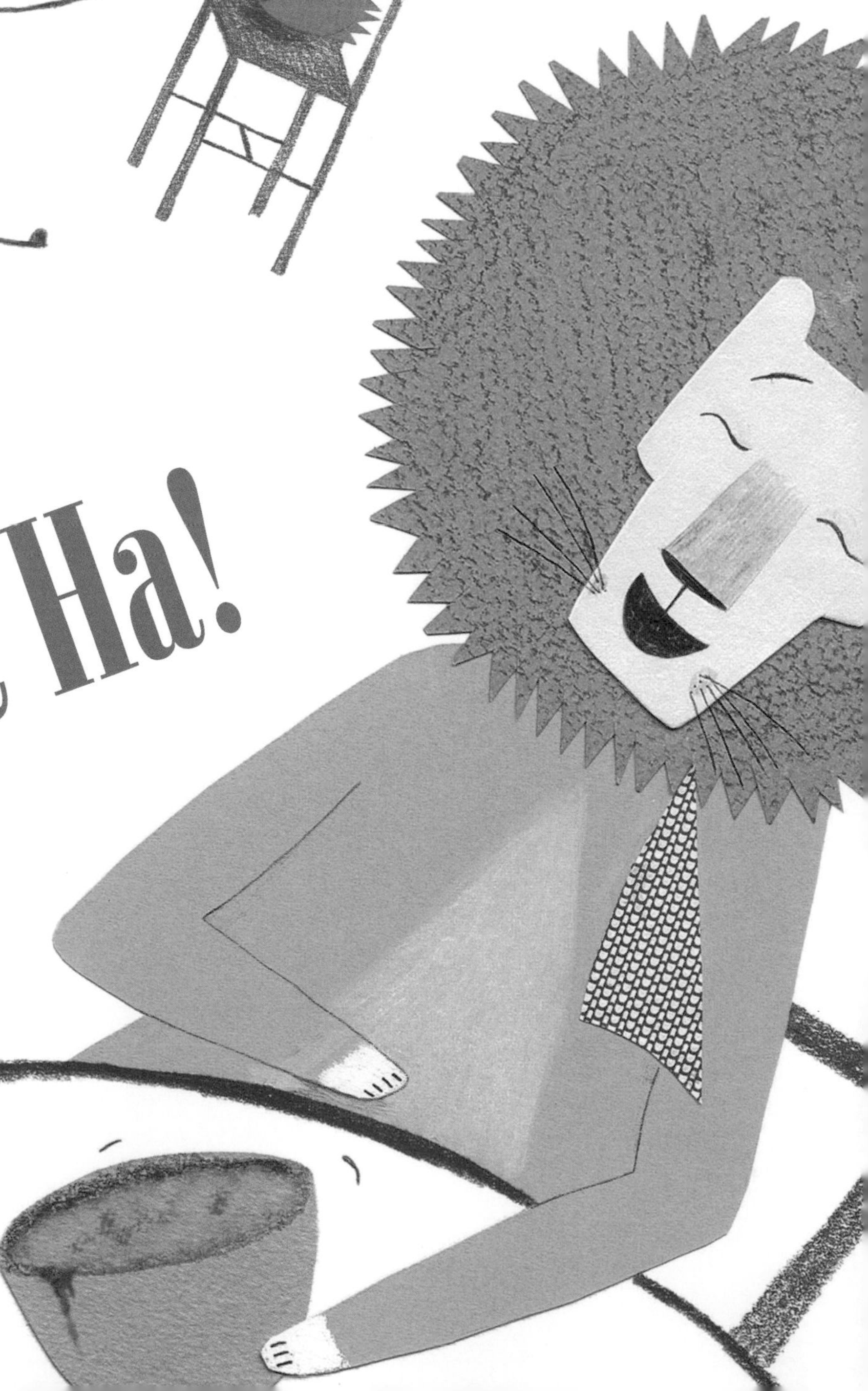

Harry gives Matt a spoon.

"You know something?" says Matt.

"What?" says Harry.

"Great

soup,

Harry!"

says Matt.

And then . . .

Harry and **soup**

If you don't have a spoon,
If you can't taste the soup,
So would I like a spoon?
Do you like the soup?
The soup is good.

The soup is good.

The soup is good.

Matt sing a
song:

you can't taste the soup.

the soup's no good.

Oh, yes, I would.

Oh, the soup is good.

The soup is good.

The soup is good.

The soup is good.

Everyone joined in,
and everyone was happy at

Happy

HARRY'S

Café.

THE END

Spiro